MW00460796

Keeping a secret has never been so hard—all Maddie wanted to do was let Cliff be the first to know they were expecting a baby!

But getting caught in a hold up at the Sip-N-Go with the Matchmakin' Posse (aka the grapevine of Mule Hollow) and two teenagers, has Maddie fighting to keep chaos from breaking out inside the convenience store. And now just getting everyone out alive is Maddie's goal. But Maddie's used to wrangling cattle and bulls into line and doing what it takes to get the job done...now, keeping three feisty, old ladies from driving the robbers to shoot them just to shut them up is proving to be a rodeo of a new kind.

Keeping her baby secret, fighting robbers, the Posse and morning sickness has Maddie unsure if she'll ever see Cliff again, much less share her secret baby news.

Don't miss story #7 in the New Horizon Ranch series. A short story involving Maddie and Cliff from book #1 in the series. If you've been hoping for baby news for them during this series you'll enjoy this quick fun read.

Maddie's Secret Baby

NEW HORIZON RANCH BOOK 6

DEBRA
CLOPTON

MADDIE'S SECRET BABY
Copyright © 2016 Debra Clopton Parks

CONTENTS

ABOUT DEBRA CLOPTON

Bestselling author Debra Clopton has sold over 2.5 million books. Her book OPERATION: MARRIED BY CHRISTMAS has been optioned for an ABC Family Movie. Debra is known for her contemporary, western romances, Texas cowboys and feisty heroines. Sweet romance and humor are always intertwined to make readers smile. A sixth generation Texan she lives with her husband on a ranch deep in the heart of Texas. She loves being contacted by readers.

Visit Debra's Website and sign up for her newsletter for news and a chance to win prizes
http://debraclopton.com

CHAPTER ONE

With her mug of coffee in hand, Maddie Masterson walked outside and leaned against the porch railing. The early morning view of her cowboy riding his horse was a beautiful sight…with the rosy pink and melon sunrise glowing behind him—it was an awe inspiring sight.

It just didn't get any better than that.

For a girl who'd had no one in her life to love until Cliff Masterson swept into her world, the sight of him always sent her heart thumping and joy cascading through her. Even after almost a year of marriage.

She sighed and murmured, "Yes ma'am, you are officially a sap over him." She sipped her coffee as peace flowed through her.

She was so blessed...

And late.

Spinning away, she hurried inside to dress for the day in tank top, jeans boots and a ponytail topped with a straw Stetson...her cowgirl uniform. She loved her life.

Her thoughts went back to Cliff and the life they were building together. She'd never forget that first day she'd met him, when he'd jumped between her and an angry bull and saved her from getting trampled.

Sparks had flown because, despite him saving her, they'd managed to get off on the wrong foot, locking horns right from the get go.

Like flint on rock went together, so did they. Goodness, they'd made sparks.

And nothing had changed about that.

They still could. Oh yes indeed, they could.

Rushing back into the kitchen, she grabbed an insulted coffee mug and filled it to the brim, then hurried back onto the porch. The sun was up now, soft and gentle, a tease before it rose to its full fury later that afternoon. It was going to be a scorcher.

"Mornin' gorgeous," Cliff called as he locked the gate and strode toward her across the yard.

Their gazes locked, and even from a hundred yards, Maddie's pulse jumped and her insides melted like butter.

He raised a hand in an easy wave. "You *sure* do look pretty in the morning light, Mrs. Masterson."

She laughed. "Now I know you're blinded by love. I'm about as plain as they come."

"Your hair could be a mess, and you could be covered in dirt," he drawled. "But darlin', you'd still be beautiful to me."

There went that melting heart again.

He made her feel beautiful no matter what she looked like. Even when she came in hot, sweaty and covered in grime after a day working cattle, he could look at her, and she felt beautiful.

"I think you're pretty, too," she teased. Her husband was one handsome, rugged male, and pretty was not a word to describe him. What that man did for a pair of chaps and a cowboy hat never ceased to amaze her.

His eyes narrowed. "You know those are fighting words."

"Oh yeah? What'ch gonna do about it?"

He smiled that crooked smile and didn't even pause as he stepped onto the porch and swept her into his arms. "Love you forever. Good morning, Mrs. Masterson," he said, then covered her mouth with his.

Maddie sighed and wrapped her arms around him and hung on. She sank into his strong arms, feeling happier and more female and desirable than she'd ever thought possible. Being a woman in a man's world wasn't easy. She wrangled cattle, used branding irons, dug post holes and built fence, among a host of other ranching jobs, so it took a lot to make her feel feminine.

Cliff Masterson had made her feel that way from the first moment they'd met.

Now Maddie's arms tightened around his neck, and she counted her blessings. This was where she was born to be, with this man forever. He kissed with a gentle yet powerful certainty that melted her insides and heated her blood. It was certainly a jumpstart to a day that gallons of caffeine could not compete with. Nothing could.

By the time he lifted his head, she could no longer think straight.

His eyes were warm as he smiled a lazy smile, straightened his hat and studied her. "It's probably a good thing you work on one ranch and I work on ours, because I might not ever get anything done. Kissing you is just too enjoyable. And more tempting than a dip in a cool creek on a hot summers day."

She chuckled. "I agree. I'm pretty partial to it."

He studied her, then suddenly his brows dipped and his gaze sharpened. "Are you feeling okay? You're pale."

"Pale? Are you kidding?" She tugged her hat off and fanned herself. "I'm probably red as a firetruck after that kiss."

He shook his head. "Nope. Pale as a piece of bread."

"You certainly know how to douse a fire. I'll

admit I'm a little tired, but it's not a big deal. I haven't been sleeping well."

"Why?"

She shrugged. "I don't know. I'll get some rest tonight. For now, I have to run. Your brother and the others are going to start thinking I'm slacking if I don't hurry."

He laughed. "Yeah, right. You know that's not true." He gave her a quick kiss on the lips and let her go. "Tonight you're getting some sleep. You've got circles under your eyes."

"Gee, thanks, buster." She glanced over her shoulder and smiled. It was nice to have someone in her life who worried about her. Until Cliff, she'd never had that.

He frowned. "I'm serious, babe. Maybe you need to take a day off. You work harder than any woman I know. You can take a day off."

"I'm fine." She climbed into her truck. "I love you and good luck. Hope you sell the horse. And drive safe delivering your bulls to the rodeo."

"Thanks. I feel good about it. I'll be on the road by noon to deliver the bulls, and if my schedule goes as planned, I'll be back here by six to fix you dinner. You can at least rest then."

She hung her head out the open window. "Thanks. We can celebrate your horse sale."

"Sounds like a plan to me." He lifted his hand in goodbye as she left.

Excitement filled her as she headed down the drive. This sale would be a lot to celebrate. Rodeo bookings for his rodeo bulls had been strong, and the cutting horse business was looking good too. The ranch might be in the black in the first year of business. She was proud for Cliff. Leaving the competitive world of bull riding at the prime of his career had been hard on him, but he'd been ready to start the next chapter of his life. She wanted this to work out for him. For them.

She couldn't wait to celebrate.

That new chapter of his life had included her and his hope--*their* hope--of a family. As she drove away, her thoughts went to another celebration she really wanted to experience with her amazing husband…having a baby.

Oh how she wanted a baby.

With Mother's Day approaching, a child of their own was heavy on her heart and mind. Growing their family weighed heavy on both of them. Every time they celebrated anything, they were also working on making their baby dream come true.

That was a win/win situation if ever there was one.

Her mouth went dry suddenly, and she felt a wave of weakness wash over her.

She'd ignored the feeling earlier, but now she acknowledged that she didn't feel exactly well. She'd been really tired the last few days, drug out with just no energy. And she'd been getting a little queasy off and on too. For a girl who was hardly ever ill, it had been an odd feeling that she'd pushed through. She didn't have time or temperament to be ill, but—

An exciting idea hit Maddie, and she straightened in the seat. Her hands gripped the steering wheel in a stranglehold. Was it possible?

Could she be pregnant?

CHAPTER TWO

P *regnant.*

Maddie stomped on the brakes and brought the truck to a screeching halt in the middle of the road. Could she be pregnant?

"Could I be?" Her heartbeat rammed her ribcage like a rhino trying to break out of a cage.

She swallowed hard as wonder overtook nausea.

"There's only one way to find out," she growled while making a U-turn in the middle of the road. Work was going to have to wait. She pressed the gas and held on.

It was time to find a pregnancy test. Now!

And she just happened to know where there was one. The new Sip-N-Go was only thirty minutes away, halfway between Mule Hollow and Ranger. The last time she'd stopped in there, she'd spotted a test kit while she was looking for a box of bandages. She remembered seeing it because her gaze had locked on the box, and that familiar yearning had gripped her so strong, she'd gotten a knot in her chest. She sure hoped it was still there. But if it wasn't, then she'd drive all the way to Ranger, which was an hour away. But she didn't care how far she had to go..

She pressed the pedal to the floorboard and sped down the country road toward the Sip-N-Go. Maybe this would be the day she would learn that she and Cliff had made a precious baby together.

Getting to the store was the longest thirty minutes Maddie had ever experienced. The pastures flew past her, but the moments ticked by like a turtle crawling backwards. *Finally*, the dull tan brick building that could potentially change her life came into view.

"Praise the good Lord," she muttered. Maddie

had wanted a family all of her life. She'd been abandoned as a baby, left sitting in her carseat at the post office. It hurt to think that someone could do that to her or any child. She knew how to love a child. How to cherish a child. And today she might learn that she'd finally learned how to make a child.

She'd begun to think that she couldn't. That something inside of her had shut down somewhere along the way and they were going to have to seek other avenues to make their baby dreams come true. But maybe not.

She leaned forward in her seat as excitement bubbled up inside her. She whipped the truck into the parking lot, drove to the vacant space and came to a jolting halt right at the front door. The jolt caused her stomach to roll and nausea rocked inside of her as she cut the motor and pushed open the door.

For the first time in her life, the very thought of tossing her cookies made her smile.

She really could be pregnant. *Hotdog, what a wonderful day.*

The parking lot was fairly vacant, which was

even better. The last thing she wanted was for someone she knew to see what she was buying. Rumors traveled like greased pigs in a small town, and she did not want Cliff to hear anything before she could tell him. Heck, someone could see her pick up the box and within minutes she could be having triplets.

Mule Hollow had a grapevine like none other.

She rushed inside and ducked around the corner of the potato chip aisle and then made a beeline to the far wall. And there it was, exactly where she'd spotted it the last time. She reached for the single box, her fingers wrapped around it, and a thrill of electricity zipped through her. *Oh please, let it be so.*

Feeling like a running back carrying a football toward the end zone, Maddie tucked the box against her midriff and headed toward the front of the store. This was going to be a hard fall if the test came up negative, but she couldn't help the excitement bursting inside of her. She wanted this so badly, it hurt, and she knew Cliff would feel the same way.

Before stepping out into the open, she peeked

over the top of the shelves. The coast was clear. She rushed toward the counter and laid the box down, then gently pushed it toward the fresh-faced teenaged boy behind the cash register. He grinned as he picked it up and studied it for a second.

He scanned the barcode. "Is this everything?" he asked.

Maddie shifted from one foot to the other and nodded.

His grin grew. "Good luck." He dropped it into a bag and held it out to her.

"Thanks. This could be my lucky day." She smiled, took the bag and started toward the doors leading outside.

"You know, our restrooms are really nice," the kid called.

Maddie stopped halfway to the doors and made her second U-turn of the day. "That's a very good idea. Thanks."

He pointed toward the sign at the back of the store, and she headed that way. This was great. She would have had a hard time waiting until she got home. Checking now would keep her from being tempted to pull off in the woods and taking the test behind a bush.

Being a country girl who rode out across the ranch working all day without the comforts of home anywhere nearby, she appreciated the cover of a thick bush. But not exactly the way she wanted to learn about a baby.

Minutes later Maddie's heart thundered as she stared at her dazed reflection in the mirror. She held the positive test in her hand. "I'm having a baby," she whispered. "*We're* having a baby," she amended, as the full impact hit her.

Once she'd been all alone in this world. Abandoned as a baby and raised in an orphanage most of her life, she'd felt alone. She'd had her friends and partners on the ranch, but until she'd met Cliff and learned to trust her feelings, there had been a hole in her heart. Now that she had Cliff to share her life with, she could not wait to tell him they were having a baby.

He was going to be so happy. Over the moon happy.

The thought of how he would react brought

tears to her eyes.

She was blinking them away when loud, excited voices sounded outside the door. The door swung open, and three women hustled into the bathroom.

Maddie's stomach dropped to her feet. Esther Mae Wilcox, Norma Sue Jenkins and Adela Green, aka "The Posse," stared at her. Maddie scrambled to hide the three inch long test, trying to stuff it in her pants, but she lost her hold and it hit the floor, the plus sign on the front was face up, proclaiming to anyone who saw it that the test had proven positive. She dropped to her knees and reached under the sink to grab it.

"*Maddie,*" Esther Mae exclaimed. "What in the world are you doin'" down there?"

"I'm, um, dropped my Chapstick," she fibbed as she managed to get the slender test tube stuffed in the waistband of her jeans. She tugged her shirt down over it and stood up. Her insides were all fluttery, but she wasn't sure if it was excitement or the sick feeling coming back.

"What are you doing here?" Norma Sue stuffed her hands to her jean clad hips.

"Honey," Adela smiled, and the sweet tiny lady came over and also gave her a hug. "Are you feeling okay? You're pale."

"You are," Esther Mae said, peering at her with apple-green eyes that stood out against her bright red hair."

"I'm fine." No way could Maddie let on to what she'd just learned. Not if she wanted Cliff to know before anyone else. These ladies had a matchmaking reputation in town, but they were also a major part of the grapevine she wanted to avoid. If they even got a hint that she was expecting, the word might be all over town by noon! And with the way gossip grew it, she'd probably be expecting triplets by the time it reached Cliff.

Nope, her lips were sealed.

"Um, what are y'all up to today?" she asked in an attempt to change the subject.

"*Road trip*," Esther Mae sang out. "You know how I love a good road trip."

Maddie chuckled. "Yes, I do. But are you sure it's not road trouble? Don't y'all tend to get into mischief when you head out of town?"

"Ha! You got thats right," Norma Sue drawled, hiking a brow toward Esther Mae. "It's her fault. Trouble follows her around like a bad tattoo."

Esther Mae's mouth dropped open before she cocked a yellow velour clad hip and slapped a hand to it. "You get into just as much as I do. Isn't that right, Adela?"

"I'm not getting into this," Adela said, her eyes twinkling as she let her friends go at it. She was the voice of reason when she needed to be, but usually she just let them go.

Norma harrumphed. "Your kind of trouble rubs off on all of us who are around you. But it should be okay today. We're just heading over to San Antonio to an art festival on the Riverwalk. Unless she falls off a sidewalk into the water, we should be okay."

"Well," Esther Mae huffed. "All I can say is I have fun. And you do too. But, girl, we had to make a pit stop. Too much coffee for me this morning."

Maddie grinned. "Me too. But I need to head to work now."

"Are you on your way to an auction?" Adela asked.

Maddie's palms dampened. "No. I just wanted a fountain drink. I kinda had a craving for a soda this morning." She groaned at her answer. Who drove thirty minutes to get a Coke before going to work? No one.

"Kind of a long drive for a Coke." Norma Sue stated the apparent.

"Yeah, but I really wanted one. Okay, gotta get to work. It was nice seeing y'all. Have a great time." Maddie moved toward the door. "And, Esther Mae, try to stay out of trouble, okay?" She winked at the redhead.

"What fun would that be?" Esther Mae chuckled. "See you later."

Maddie waved, then headed out the restroom door and into the store. She paused and breathed a sigh of relief. She'd made it. Now to just get to Cliff and tell him the good news. She rounded the corner, determined to get through that front door before the Posse came out of the restroom. She cast a glance over her shoulder and then toward the boy behind the counter. A bulky, ponytailed guy stood beside him.

And he held a handgun on the teen.

Maddie gasped and jerked to a stop as the thug turned his gun on her.

"Stop!" he snapped, his eyes glittering as his hand tightened on the revolver.

The teen paused from digging money out of the register and stuffing it in a bag. He stared at her with remarkably calm eyes. Sweat dampened his forehead as his eyes met and held hers.

"Get over there," the robber demanded, jabbing the gun toward the front.

Maddie's entire body stiffened as her hand went to her stomach…her baby. The feel of the test cylinder against her skin reminded her of how much she needed this trouble to go away.

"Do it! Or you'll wish you had," Ponytail growled.

A second man, this one holding a shotgun, moved into view. "I'd do as you're told, or you'll pay."

Don't lose your head. Keep cool.

Maddie had faced down two thousand pound bulls and won. And right now the cowgirl in her wanted to kick these thugs' butts like a two-hundred-fifty-pound bouncer taking out troublemakers on a Saturday night bar fight. For a girl used to making her way in a man's world, Maddie did not take lightly to being pushed around. She didn't really have a fear monitor because she'd never really had anything to lose...until now.

But then again, she had a baby on board, and protective instincts like nothing she'd ever felt before had her gaze narrowing, and her hand balling into a fist.

Stand down, Maddie. Stand down, girl. Let the jerks take the money and get out of here.

The tiny voice of reason was right. What could she do anyway? They had guns, and she had nothing. Her voice of reason was talking sense. The sooner they were gone, the quicker she could get home and tell Cliff their beautiful news.

"Move," Ponytail yelled, breaking into her thoughts.

Maddie's pulse raced as she moved on around the edge of the front row to where the second man pointed his shotgun. Racing pulse and nausea were not a good combination.

Maddie gasped when she saw a teenage girl standing where the thug was pointing his shotgun. She was hunched into herself and crying softly. Now she looked at Maddie with terror in her big brown eyes. Instant fury washed through Maddie, adding to the calamity of things going on inside of her. Her stomach rolled, but she fought the feeling as she went to stand beside the girl.

"It's going to be all right," she said quietly, giving the girl a quick side-armed hug. Maddie prayed she was right.

The girl sniffed but said nothing.

Maddie glared from one man to the other, wanting to whack the two dirt bags with something hard. Her stomach had other ideas as it rolled and felt oddly shaky. Like low blood sugar. She'd had feelings similar to this a few times when she'd worked long hours and not taken the time to eat. But the rolling stomach was different. Cheese crackers were stuffed in the front rack at the end of the shelf. Maddie snatched a package from its perch, hoping food would help settle everything down.

The girl hiccupped and watched her with disbelieving eyes. She was probably wondering how Maddie could eat at a time like this.

"Sorry, low blood sugar," Maddie whispered, and crammed a cracker into her mouth and chewed. Her mouth went dry and--ugh! This feeling was not good! "I need a Coke," she told thug number two.

He glared at her. "What?"

Sweat popped across her forehead. "I'm feeling a little sick. I need a Coke, a soda to settle my stomach."

Both men gaped at her, but she was now desperate. "It's either let me have a Cokek or I'm tossing my cookies right here in the middle of your robbery. Not the coolest thing on the block."

Ponytail's eyes narrowed, and she figured she'd just pushed her luck and was about to bite the bullet. But hey, it was what it was, and she returned his glare as steady as she could manage.

"Get the Coke," he growled. "But make it quick, or it won't matter if you're sick or not."

Maddie scooted around to the glass enclosure and grabbed a plastic bottle from inside. She twisted the lid off and took a sip, breathing steady breaths and praying again that everything would settle down. She really needed her wits about her. She took another sip and a small bite of cracker. Things eased back a bit, and she walked back around the corner to stand beside the girl.

Shotgun dude just stared at her as she sipped her Coke.

"Is this all there is?" Ponytail demanded, glaring at the kid, drawing Maddie's attention back to the counter, where some cash lay.

"That's it, I swear," the kid said, his voice shaking.

Maddie considered what might happen if this holdup did not go well. The jerk pointed the gun at the teen, then at the door behind him. "What's in there?"

"The manager's office." The teens gaze shot to the young girl, and Maddie saw a flicker of…protectiveness in his young eyes. He pulled his shoulders back and suddenly looked taller.

Maddie groaned. They did not need any teenage-impress-the-girl hero scenarios right now. She did not want to see anyone get hurt.

Right now they needed calm, rational thinking.

"Open the door," demanded Ponytail.

"Okay, but I don't know the combo to the safe," the teen declared.

"Safe? Bingo." Ponytail shot a grin at his buddy, who was shifting from one foot to the other next to the glass front door. His own gun was pointed toward Maddie and the girl, and she hoped he didn't accidently pull the trigger.

She sipped more Coke, thankful for the miracle effect of the drink and crackers on upset stomachs. Things were getting a little better. Then she heard laughter and chatter.

Oh no! The ladies were coming out of the restroom.

Maddie had forgotten they were back there. Her gaze swung toward the sound of their voices, then back toward the robbers. How were they going to react?

Ponytail and Doorman both glared in the direction of the chatter. The ladies were out of sight still but everyone could hear them advancing up the row.

"Norma Sue," Esther Mae called, laughing. "You've got toilet paper stuck to the bottom of your boot, and it flaps every time you take a step."

"Well, for crying loud," Norma Sue snapped. "There, it's off," the robust ranch woman replied as she came barreling around the end of the shelving unit. Instantly she saw the guns and came to a jolting halt. "What in the tarnation?"

Esther Mae ran into her backside. "*Norm*- What is *wrong* with you?" the excitable red head asked, then stuck her head around her friend. Her green eyes nearly popped out of their sockets. "A holdup," she shrieked. "It's a holdup!"

"What?" Adela poked her white head around her friend's elbow and gasped.

Ponytail pointed his gun at them, and Maddie started praying again as she saw Norma Sue's eyes narrow.

Coke and crackers were not going to fix this. What they needed was a *real* miracle.

CHAPTER THREE

"A hold up! It's a holdup!" Esther Mae continued shrieking, her face turning beet red.

"As if it's not obvious," Norma Sue barked, glaring at Ponytail with challenge in her alert eyes as she roared, "Get a grip, Esther Mae. Can't you see they've got guns?"

"But...but—"

"Esther." Maddie interjected because Norma Sue's attention had locked onto the thugs like seeker missiles. Fear raced through Maddie because this holdup had just morphed into another dimension, and Maddie had to get a handle on her friends before Ponytail freaked out and started shooting them all.

"Now, girls." Adela chimed in, always the voice of reason. Maddie was glad to have help wrangling this runaway rodeo into a corral. The tiny woman stepped around her friends and smiled sweetly and serenely at the thugs. The small woman with enough grace for a nation and the voice of an angel. "These young men must be in very bad need of *something* if they are resorting to armed robbery."

I'll give them something, Maddie almost muttered aloud as she shot a glare of her own at Ponytail.

He was frowning. "Yeah, I need something, all right. The money. Now you old biddies get over there with the other two, or I'll take out the redhead just for the fun of it."

"Well," Esther Mae huffed, and her face grew redder than her hair. "What would your mama say about this." She harrumphed and got a reverse elbow to the ribs from Norma Sue.

"Zip it, Esther," Norma gritted out of the side of her mouth, like everyone in the joint couldn't hear her. "He wants to shoot you."

Maddie felt it a good time to intervene. "Why don't you ladies do what they say and join me over here? Esther Mae, come here," she urged, motioning with her hand. "Now," she snapped when no one moved.

"Yes, that sounds like a perfectly lovely idea," Adela agreed, daring to hike a perfect brow at Ponytail as she gently stepped behind her friends and pushed them from the back. "*March*, girls. We'll have no shootings today."

It was the first time Maddie had ever heard Adela raise her voice. If this firm enunciation of the demand could be considered raised. Maybe firm was more like it. Whatever it was, Esther Mae and Norma Sue complied.

Maddie breathed a momentary sigh of relief as her friends joined her beside the endless rack of chewing gum. Esther Mae stood next to the sleeves of gumballs. Giant gumballs and medium gumballs. Norma Sue had Juicy Fruit at her shoulder, and Adela stood beside the endless line of flavored bubble gum.

Maddie's mind raced. There were as many possibilities of something going terribly wrong in this scenario as there were endless flavors of gum on the rack behind the Posse.

What could she do?

It was broad daylight.

This was a busy place despite being in the middle of nowhere, and someone was bound to drive up at any given moment, and what was going to happen then?

"Open the door," Ponytail demanded again and poked the teen in the ribs a second time. "Deek, you keep them in line out here," he called to Doorman.

So Deek was one of their names. Maddie glanced at the man then back at the lanky teen as he took a breath and, to his credit, kept his head as he pushed opened the door and stepped to the side. "There you go. Knock yourself out, dude."

"Boy, that'd be a blessing if he knocked himself out." Norma Sue grunted and met Maddie's gaze with a calculating look.

Maddie was struggling with the need to do something, and she could see in the older cowgirl's eyes that she was having the same struggle. They were both used to rolling up their sleeves and getting the job done. No backing down and letting things go awry. But this was different. And though Maddie's stomach had calmed down some, the feel of the pregnancy test was still making an imprint against her skin. She had a baby on board.

Esther Mae snatched a sleeve of colorful, giant gumballs from the rack and drew the attention of Deek. He frowned.

"Sorry, I'm nervous," she squeaked and began trying to open the gum.

Deek shifted his glare to the door his friend had gone. "Come on, Simon. Let's go."

Esther Mae tore open the gum and several pieces flew out, hit the floor and rolled across the tiles. She managed to hang onto a big red gumball and stuffed it into her mouth and began chewing like there was no tomorrow. Maybe there wasn't.

Adela moved to stand by the crying girl. "Honey, it's going to be just fine. You need to calm down. God's in control of this."

Maddie let Adela take over consoling the girl.

She'd be better at it. Maddie needed to concentrate on how to get out of this because, yes, God was in control, but she felt like she was part of his plan to get that control. Either that or she was just too blamed nosey for her own good and might very well wreck His plan. If that was the case, then hopefully He had a backup plan.

Her thoughts shifted back to the baby growing inside of her, and her stomach began to churn again. She willed herself to relax.

To let the tense, volatile moment pass. It had to. They'd all walk out of here, and she'd be in Cliff's arms tonight celebrating their child.

Everyone just had to remain calm.

When his phone rang, Cliff was pulling out of the drive heading toward New Horizon Ranch hauling the large cattle trailer loaded with professional bucking bulls. He'd sold the horse for a full price, which was a big score for them. He couldn't wait until tonight to share the news with Maddie. Plus he wanted to see her before he left town. He couldn't shake the need to make sure she was all right. She just hadn't looked well this morning, and that wasn't like Maddie.

She was a hard worker, with a tough exterior and healthy as they came. Her level of physical exercise probably contributed to that. But Maddie was also sweet and gentle, and there was a part of her that not everyone saw, the tender woman who'd been hurt by life and lack of love. She'd filled his world with more love than he'd ever thought possible, and his only true desire in life was to give as much back to her as she'd given to him. But lately, she'd seemed preoccupied...even a little sad when she thought he wasn't looking.

And he knew what it was, and it was starting to kill him that he wasn't giving her what she needed, what she'd always wanted more than anything. A child.

In the year they'd been married he'd come to know her almost as well as he knew himself. She was his wife, and everything about his wife interested him. She'd been alone all her life. Abandoned as a child, she'd learned to guard her heart, and when he'd met her, it had taken some work on his part to tear those walls down. He loved her with all his heart, and he'd give her anything. But he'd begun to think he wasn't going to be able to give his amazing wife her heart's desire. They'd been trying to start a family almost from the beginning of their marriage. He'd wanted a family too, but Maddie's desire went far deeper than most. She longed for the family that she'd never had, and he longed to give her one. But it wasn't happening.

And he was afraid she was starting to draw into herself, question if she deserved a family. Because he knew she'd thought she hadn't deserved love. But they'd overcome that issue.

And they would overcome this.

He just needed to talk to her. He'd needed to do it sooner but had hoped things would get better.

Today, halfway through the sale of the quarter horse, he'd had the strongest need to see her. To touch her, to hold her. And there was no way he was waiting till tonight. The bulls would get delivered, but he was seeing Maddie first.

When his phone rang, the need twisted inside of

him, and he had the strangest feeling that something wasn't right.

The ID showed Brady Cannon's number. Sheriff Brady Cannon.

His heart began pounding irrationally as he punched the button. "Brady, what's up?"

"Cliff, no time to waste. You need to keep your head on straight, but we got an alert that there was a holdup going down at the Sip-N-Go, and so, though we haven't yet made our presence known, we're about to…." He paused and a knot lodged in Cliff's throat. "Cliff, we've checked out all the license plates of the cars in the parking lot, and Maddie's truck is one of them. We're probably looking at a hostage situation."

No way. "A hostage situation?" His words came out as if he were in a hollow drum.

"Yeah, and the tags also came back on Norma Sue's truck."

"But Maddie? She left for work. What's she doing twenty miles from town at a convenience store? No. She had no reason—"

"Cliff, her truck is parked right in front of the

building. We've run her license. It's her truck."

His mouth went dry. His foot eased up on the gas pedal, and he coasted down the road with the cattle behind him. "I…" *Get a grip, Masterson.* He sucked in a breath. "I'm on my way. You don't let anything happen to her." The words came out stiff, as he found it hard to speak.

Maddie was his life.

"That's our plan. But there's more. Norma Sue's in there too, and Esther Mae and Adela are with her. With Maddie's take-charge tendencies and Norma Sue's…it could be majorly volatile inside there right now. Throw in Esther Mae, and there is no calculating what we're up against."

Cliff's blood chilled. His wife was used to taking care of herself. His wife wasn't afraid of much and had strong protective instincts. Brady had it right. This was not good in so many more ways than just the obvious.

CHAPTER FOUR

Shifty-eyed Deek was getting more nervous by the moment.

Maddie watched him as he watched them and the window. She moved beside the others and tried to keep her mouth shut.

Instead of disappearing, the tension in the small store had only grown tighter as the moments ticked by. Maddie had finally realized that the reason no one new had stopped in was because there was no traffic on the two-lane road out front. But why?

She was fighting the ups and down of nausea, feeling more like she was on a storm-tossed boat at sea instead of in a convenience store in the middle of Texas pastureland.

"Maddie, you look positively green." Esther Mae whispered. "Are you feeling bad?"

"I'm fine. I'm feeling a little sick, but I'll make it. That's what the Coke is for." She had set the drink on the shelf beside them within easy access when she needed it. "I'm thinking if we let them have what they want, they'll leave."

"Not what I'm thinking," Norma Sue ground out through the side of her mouth. "We've seen their faces. That means we could all be in major trouble if they realize they won't be able to hide once we describe them to the police."

Maddie hadn't wanted to voice that concern, but of course Norma Sue would have thought of that.

Esther Mae nodded and chomped her gum. "I think we need to take them down. We can do this, girls."

Maddie and Norma Sue stared at the red head-the *hot*-head.

"We can," she said, as if defending her claim. "We just need a plan." She was talking so low they almost couldn't hear her.

"I've been thinking that too," Maddie said. "But someone...or all of us could get hurt."

"That's right," Norma Sue said. "That's why I'm going to do this, and y'all are going to get behind that shelf when I give you the signal."

"Ha," Esther Mae grunted.

"No way," Maddie agreed. "We'll do this together."

Adela scooted near. "I'll help too."

"You'll take care of the girl, and that's enough," Norma Sue said. "And pray."

Earlier Ponytail, or Simon as his buddy had called him, had shoved the clerk, Jessie, away and told him to get with the others while he disappeared into the room with the safe. The teen wasted no time hurrying to where they stood. Immediately the girl, Lizzie, fell into his arms, and they'd hugged hard. Lizzie had told Adela that Jessie was seventeen, and she was sixteen, and that they'd been dating for about six months. And that she loved him. Now the two were holding onto each other in the background. Maddie did not want Jessie trying to be a hero for Lizzy.

Adela studied them, then nodded at Maddie and her two buddies. "Think it through. Don't be rash. There's a lot at stake here."

Norma Sue nodded and her expression hardened like a gunslinger about to have a shootout in the center of town. And that look had Maddie's stomach churning like a washing machine on high speed.

"What are y'all talking about over there?" Deek snapped and Maddie worried that Simon would hear him and come out of the back room. They had heard him back there cursing and she didn't figure things were going well with the safe.

"Um, I'm still not feeling well," Maddie said. It was the first thing that came to mind, and it was the truth.

"That's right," Esther Mae declared. "Look at her. She's greener than a toad frog on a lily-pad."

Deek's eyes narrowed. "I don't care. Be quiet."

Norma Sue was staring at her with wide eyes. "Are you *pregnant*?"

That was not the question she wanted to answer.

She was trying to decide what to say when an odd, loud whump, whump, whump sound from outside drew everyone's focus. Maddie spun toward the windows just as news helicopter lowered over the parking lot and hovered just outside the windows.

"Simon, get out here!" Deek yelled, dancing in front of the glass as if not certain whether to run or stay.

Maddie saw the chopper and then three sheriff SUV's and a cop car wheel into the parking lot. The helicopter lifted and pulled back to hover a ways back while the law enforcement vehicles slid to a halt at odd angles, passengers' sides facing the store. They'd made a barricade. Officers jumped out and aimed guns across the vehicles toward the building.

Maddie was too stunned to move. And momentarily so was everyone inside the building. Except for dancing Deek. He looked like he was the one who was going to be sick.

Everything happened in a matter of seconds. And Maddie focused as dread instead of relief filled her. This could be horrible.

"You're surrounded," someone yelled through a

megaphone. "Come out with your hands up."

"What the--" Simon spat out as he raced from the back room. "You," he yelled at Jessie. "Get over here."

"No," Lizzy cried, clinging to her boyfriend.

"Shh, stop crying, Lizzy. I love you." Jessie disengaged himself from her, shooting Maddie a glance he strode back across the room and around the counter.

Simon yanked the teen in front of him.

"That's Brady!" Esther Mae exclaimed and started tossing giant gumballs into her mouth again.

Sheriff Brady Cannon. Maddie thought as she glanced around at her friends. She could see their fear escalating like a roaring wildfire.

"This is bad," Deek whined, halting his stutter-stepping. "Really bad, Simon!"

Simon grabbed Jessie's collar and yanked him closer. "Everybody get back."

Maddie bristled, not liking the way Simon was treating Jessie. She also didn't plan on letting anything happen to the kid. Young love was sweet, and Maddie had no plans for Lizzy and Jessie's love story to end today.

Her palms started sweating. She had to do something. This situation with Brady and his men coming to their rescue should have reassured her. It didn't. There were TV helicopters out there. Who knew what they were going to do. Turn it into a circus? With the potential of turning into a disaster?

Simon's face was molten red with fury.

"You're surrounded," Brady called again. "Come out with your hands up."

"Yeah, sure," Simon yelled, making Lizzie jump and Esther Mae choke on her gum.

Norma Sue started beating Esther Mae on the back and starring at Maddie with squinted eyes. "You okay, Esther?" she yelled, as if Esther Mae was hard a hearing instead of choking.

"I'm fine," she wheezed. "I didn't swallow it. Thank goodness."

"We got to get out of here," Deek yelled at his partner.

"Now, son," Norma Sue barked. "Don't go gettin' all flustered. You do not want to harm anyone in this building."

"That's right," Maddie agreed. "Give yourselves up, and this won't go as badly as it could. You haven't hurt anyone."

"Yet," Simon yelled and waved his gun as he tightened his hold on Jessie. "But I will. And, lady, I'm not your son."

"That's for doggone sure." Norma Sue cocked her white Stetson head to the side and glared at him. "Because if you were my son, I'd have you laid over my knee and I'd be whupping the tarnation out of your sorry backside."

"She would too," Esther Mae tossed out indignantly.

Simon leveled his gun on Esther Mae. "Lady, I'm already tired of you."

Maddie stepped between everyone. "Hold on. Don't do anything crazy." Her hand remained on her stomach, and she prayed her little baby would forgive her if she messed up. Because there was no way she was letting these hotheads hurt her friends.

"Stop right where you are," Simon snapped. He pointed his gun at her stomach, then rammed it back into Jessie's ribs. "Or do you want me to shoot this one?"

Fury swept over Maddie.

"He's going to hurt, Jessie," the girl whimpered and turned her tear-stained face to Adela's shoulder. Adela wrapped her arms around the girl and did what she did best, gave comfort while her electric blue eyes met Maddie's. "Everyone needs to be calm," she urged in her sweet, steady voice.

Maddie nodded at Adela, getting the message that passed between the two of them. They had to keep it calm. They had to get everyone through this. But that was easier thought then done.

"I'm fine, Lizzie," Jessie grunted, his voice steady considering the facts.

Thankfully, Jessie appeared to be the third calm one in the room, a good thing since more sirens sounded outside and chaos seemed about to break out inside.

CHAPTER FIVE

Cliff had barely hung up from talking to the Sheriff when he saw lights flashing in his rearview mirror and heard the blaring sirens of the Mule Hollow Fire Department. His phone started ringing. He kept his foot on the gas an pressed the button again.

"Yeah," he snapped, not wasting any time on preliminaries.

"We're coming up on you." It was Rafe. His twin was a volunteer with the fire department, as were most men from the ranch and from town. In a small community like theirs that was mostly pasturelands, grass fires were a major hazard. Everyone pitched in and did their share helping out. And the volunteer fire department also helped out in emergency situations if called on.

"Y'all going to be backup at the Sip-N-Go?" he asked.

"Yeah. Brady called and said we were needed. Going to take over traffic control at least, so the law can deal with the situation and not the blockade on this side. He said there was a hostage situation."

"Maddie's one of them." The words fell from his lips like cement off a cliff.

"What did you say?"

"You heard me. I thought she was at work."

There was a pause on the other end of the line. "She didn't show up. I didn't think anything about it because I thought she might be helping you. I knew you had a load of bulls to deliver. Brady said she's in there? He didn't tell us anything. Just told us to come. Man, this isn't good."

"She's got a good head on her shoulders." The statement was more to reassure himself than it anything. They all knew she had a great head on her shoulders.

"Yeah, she does. We're all here, and we'll do whatever it takes to get her out of there."

He knew by "all," Rafe was talking about her partners from the ranch. Ty, Dalton, Chase and Rafe. It was reassuring to know he had backup. That Maddie had backup.

"How are you?"

The truck reached the back of the cattle trailer, but Cliff didn't move over. He wasn't planning on slowing down on the shoulder for anyone. "I've got to get to her."

"You will, buddy. Lead on. We've got your back. But remember Brady knows what he's doing."

"Yeah, but he's not in control of what's going down inside that building." And that worried Cliff the most. There were a lot of loose cannons inside right now, and he wasn't talking about the robbers.

"Look what you got me into," Deek accused Simon over the whump, whump of the helicopter and the screeching of brakes on pavement as more cop cars rolled to a halt in the parking lot.

Maddie watched the two robbers fight between

themselves. *Robbers, helicopters, police. And she'd just wanted to take a pregnancy test, for crying out loud.*

And now she just wanted to tell her husband he was going to be a daddy.

"You didn't have to come along. Stop freaking out and move away from the window, or you might get a bullet. Either that, or grab one of the women and use her for cover."

"What?" Esther Mae gasped. "You are the rudest man!"

Maddie spun toward the redhead. "Hush, Esther Mae. Are you kidding me?"

"I have to agree with Esther Mae," Norma Sue said and squared her shoulders. "I'm about tired of these two scaring the kids."

"You're surrounded. Let the hostages go," Brady demanded over the megaphone.

"Does he think I'm stupid," Simon snarled.

Well, yeah. Duh. Maddie resisted the urge to voice her opinion.

"There's a lot of vehicles out there," Deek said, peeking over the top of the shelves, where he'd finally rushed, thankfully not taking one of them with him as a hostage. "You didn't say anything about us getting shot!"

"Shut up, Deek."

"We should have grabbed the money and left. But you just had to see in that safe."

The phone rang. Both men froze and stared at it.

"Maybe y'all should get that," Norma Sue snapped.

"Yeah, and let us go." Esther Mae's voice was high pitched.

Lizzie's crying started again.

"There, there," Adela soothed. "You have to stop crying, honey. Jessie's not crying. He's being very brave."

And he was. The kid was quietly taking in everything, Maddie realized.

"Pick it up, guys," he urged. "They probably want to offer you a getaway car and a million bucks or something."

Maddie dropped her chin to her chest and sighed. Jessie didn't need to put a dollar number in their heads. If these guys asked for a million bucks, they were all sunk.

"You could ask for a car, for sure," she offered, her head lifting as she spoke. "In trade for us."

Simon stared at her, then pointed the gun at her. "You. Get over here." He pointed at the phone. "Pick it up."

Maddie did as she was told. "Hello." Her voice cracked as she spoke.

"Who is speaking?"

She didn't recognize the voice on the other end of the line. "Maddie Masterson. Who is this?"

"Austin Drake, ma'am. I'm a new deputy in Mule Hollow. We're going to get y'all out of there."

She heard someone in the background ask him who'd answered the call.

"It's Maddie Masterson," the deputy answered, then asked her, "How are you?" His deep voice pulsed with concern. "Are you and the other hostages all right?"

"We're all okay. But stressed, as you can imagine." *And the Posse is getting a little unpredictable.*

"We're going to get you out. How many hostages are there, and how many assailants are there?"

"Two of them and six of us--"

"Don't tell him that." Simon punched her in the shoulder with his revolver, knocking her back. She took the blow with a grunt as pain exploded through her arm.

"Maddie, what happened?"

"Nothing," she said. "Hang on." She glared at Simon. "What do you want me to tell the deputy?"

"We want a car," Simon snarled, starting to look a little like a caged animal.

"A fast car," Deek added, pacing again.

"And we want a million dollars, like the kid here said," Simon demanded.

Maddie rubbed her forehead. "You might want to be realistic. It'll take them forever to get that kind of money together. If they're even willing to pay that for us." What was she doing?

"She's right. We just came in here to rob a cash register, man." Deek looked panicked.

He was sweating, and Maddie almost felt sorry for him. Talk about ruining your life just because you followed the wrong person down the wrong path.

"Fine. Two hundred and fifty thousand. They

can get that. And it'd better be fast."

Maddie relayed the message to Austin. It was all she could do. She wished so desperately that she could talk to Cliff one more time. She felt like the world was on her shoulders as she looked across the room at her friends and the teens.

"We'll get back to you, Maddie. Hang in there and keep calm. And alive."

"Hang up," Simon demanded. "Tell them to call back when they've got our demands met. And it better be soon."

"He's told me to hang up," she told Austin.

"Now," Simon yelled.

"Please tell my husband, Cliff, I'm fine," she managed before Simon grabbed the phone and punch the button himself. Her heart clutched painfully with love for Cliff as the phone was wrenched from her grasp.

"How did they know we were here?" Simon yelled.

Maddie wondered why it had taken him so long to realize that someone or something had to have alerted the law.

Simon glared at Jessie. "You. What did you do?"

"Nothing man, nothing."

Simon pointed his gun at Jessie. "Did you punch a button or something?"

Maddie saw the truth in the kid's eyes as they met hers. He had definitely done something. There must be a button somewhere near the register, and he'd pushed it.

She had to do something now or they were going to hurt him. "It doesn't matter," she said, desperate to pull attention off of Jessie. "Someone was bound to alert them sooner or later."

His eyes narrowed. "Was it you—"

Norma Sue stepped forward. "What do you fellas do when you're not holding up the Sip-N-Go?"

All eyes turned to the stout ranch woman.

"*What?*" Simon stared at Norma Sue like she'd lost her marbles.

Maddie was going to lose hers crackers and her mind! What was Norma Sue doing?

Norma Sue pushed her Stetson off her forehead. Her kinky grey curls poked out from under it as she hiked a brow and met Simon's glare. "You know," she said conversationally. "Like do you ride horses? Motorcycles? Do you like to read?"

"Or *knit?*" Esther Mae quipped, drawing odd looks from everyone. She shrugged and squeaked, "Well, some people like to knit."

Silence filled the room.

Maddie was fretting over trying to keep everyone safe, not letting anything happen to anyone inside this building, and Norma Sue and Esther Mae were not helping.

But the wacky redhead's goofball question had stumped the robbers.

And then Deek lifted his hand. "I do kind of like it," he said, with a sheepish expression. "My grandma used to teach me."

"Aw, man, don't go there." Simon groaned. "Get some pride. *Knitting?* You're robbing a store, not at a knitting class."

Deek's jaw flinched as he glared at Simon. "I got pride, you know. Don't tell me what to do. You got me into this."

"Dude, stop listening to that silly old dingbat

redhead. You ain't no knitter."

Adela stepped forward and smiled at Deek. "That sounds like you had a very nice time with your grandmother." She looked at Simon. "Did you do anything with your grandmother?"

Simon scowled deeper. "*No.* I never had a grandmother."

"Oh, I'm so sorry," Adela said, genuine compassion in her words. "Did you do anything nice with your mother?"

"Lady, I didn't have a mother either. I take care of myself. Now can we stop with the family reunion?"

Norma scowled. "Maddie didn't have family either. And she didn't resort to a life of crime."

Okay, so much for distracting them.

Then again, they were distracted, because Maddie realized suddenly that the tough as bootstrap cattlewoman had maneuvered herself to stand beside Deek, and he was too preoccupied with being mad at Simon to care.

And Esther Mae, silly dingbat, as Simon had called her, just kept on being a dingbat.

"Knitting," Esther Mae continued, "doesn't mean you're a wimp. Oh, no, it does not. There are really smart, manly men who knit."

Maddie zoned out on the conversation as her mind turned over the trouble they were in. Her gut told her that it was time to do something. If that car drove up and they took her, one of the Posse, or one of these kids as hostage, she felt certain that someone would get hurt. Maybe killed.

She knew Norma Sue was thinking the same thing. Maddie had placed herself between the robbers and Adela and Esther Mae. And those two had moved in front of the teens. And since Norma Sue had eased from beside Maddie so that she was now as close to Deek as she could get it appeared plans were being made and she better get on board with them.

And obviously the plan left Maddie with Simon.

CHAPTER SIX

The Sip-N-Go came into view in the distance. The road had been barricaded a good distance away from the store. Cliff pressed the brakes and slowed the truck down to a halt behind the line of vehicles that were waiting for the trouble to clear so they could get on with their day. Groups had gathered outside their cars for a better look.

Two news helicopters from surrounding larger towns hovered above the area, and various types of law enforcement vehicles angled across the parking lot of the store. It looked like a scene he'd witnessed in movies countless times but had never expected to see anywhere near his small town. And not with his wife involved.

He jumped from his truck and jogged toward the barricade.

"I need to get by here," he told the two lawmen. "My wife is in there."

"Are you Cliff Masterson?"

He nodded.

"Stay low and find Sheriff Brady. They're waiting on you."

"Hey, I'm his brother," Rafe called as he jogged up and stopped beside him. "We're here to help if y'all need it." He waved a hand at the men from New Horizon Ranch and others who had arrived in the emergency vehicles. "They'll do whatever y'all need. I'm with him." He put a hand on Cliff's shoulder.

"Stay low. I'll radio you're coming."

Cliff could make out the forms of several people moving around inside the building. Brady waved him over.

"We're getting ready to make a call. Hold on, Cliff. Rafe, keep him calm. And when you see Hank,

Roy Don and Sam come up, hold them back too. They're going to be worried about their wives also."

"You got it," Rafe said.

"I'm not going to just stand here--" Cliff said.

"Right now you are." Brady's expression was firm. "Let us do our job. The robbers have demanded a car and money, and we have the car on its way."

Cliff grabbed his arm. "Get her out of there."

"We're going to do everything we can to get them all out of there." Brady gave him a compassionate nod and then went back to the other officers.

It was all Cliff could do to keep his boots planted to the pavement. He turned to Rafe. "They won't go without a hostage." He stared after Brady. It was all he could do to keep his voice steady as anguish and rage battled together inside of him.

"Probably not," Rafe agreed, grim-faced as their gazes locked.

Cliff's heart felt like a steel band was cranking down around it. He yanked his hat off and rammed a hand through his hair. "I need to get to Maddie. I am not going to stand by and wait for there to be a chance of her being in that car when it drives off. Someone's going to get caught in the crossfire somewhere down the road when the car comes face to face with a barricade." He knew Maddie. She was a protector. A take charge person who would put everyone else above herself. And the Posse was in there with her. "You know her, Rafe. She'll do everything she can to get the others out. If there's any way at all, she'll make sure she's the hostage they take." And as much as he hated the thought, it was also one of the many reasons he loved her.

And he wasn't ready or planning to lose her.

Maddie had been going over the options in her head. Deek had moved away from Norma Sue, and he and Simon were now huddled up talking. They were arguing.

"Can you disable Simon long enough for me to get Deek's gun when he gets near me?" Norma Sue whispered.

"This isn't a good idea," Maddie whispered back.

She didn't want to point out that Deek was in his twenties and Norma was in her sixties. And there were guns involved. "Someone's going to get hurt."

"Not if I can help it," Norma Sue said. "If someone gets in that car with them, it's not going to be good, and you know it. And I know you, Maddie Masterson. You're planning on being that person."

She had Maddie on that. No way was she letting anyone else in that car if she could help it.

"I've wrangled more ornery cattle than most cowboys, and I can flip one faster than cowboys half my age. I can take that puny thug out and not even break a sweat. So I'm doing this. Are you with me? Can you take out Simon?"

Maddie knew she had to have faith in the ranch woman. "I can do it."

A familiar wide grin spread across her face. "I knew you could. Ranching builds strong muscle, and you're the best ranch woman I've ever known."

Coming from Norma Sue, that was an amazing compliment since she was legendary in these parts. "Thank you. I feel the same about you."

"Then you be ready for the signal, and we'll have

us one heck of a rodeo."

Maddie almost smiled. She had no plans to let this get to that point. Her stomach rolled again, and she clamped her hand down on it and willed the relentless nausea to back down as she asked, "What's the signal?"

"You'll know it when you see it."

The phone rang before Maddie could ask for more clarification. Immediately Simon yelled for her to get back to the phone. She grabbed the Coke and took a swig as she moved back to the phone. Simon came to stand next to her. The gun was at his side, but he didn't jab her in the ribs. Maybe he was starting to get comfortable. To believe that the little women were not going to ruffle his feathers. She planned to pluck his feathers.

Deek hovered between Simon and Norma Sue. And she saw Norma ease closer to him.

"Answer it, Maddie," Esther Mae urged. "I bet they've got a car. And it's about time, too. I'm about to pee in my pants. You know my bladder is not what it used to be, and we've been standing here far too long."

Simon and Deek both glared at her.

Her green eyes widened innocently. "Well, it's not. I'm old, you know, and I do not know how y'all are going this long without visiting the little boys' room. Because I'm suffering. I truly am."

"Shut your trap, woman," Simon yelled. "You are driving me nuts."

Esther Mae jutted out a canary yellow covered hip and chomped her gum. Making popping noises as she did. "You sound just like my Hank. I will admit that I can drive a man to drink. Not that my Hank drinks, but he says he should."

"I feel sorry for him."

The phone continued to ring as Simon stared at Esther Mae, probably contemplating shooting her right then and there.

"Okay, I'm picking the phone up," Maddie said, hoping to defuse the situation.

"Yeah, and they better have our car." Simon glared at her.

Deek had started pacing erratically back and forth beside Norma Sue, his gun hanging at his side half the time.

Maddie picked up the phone. "Maddie here."

"We're bringing in the car."

"They're bringing the car," she relayed.

"Maddie, we've met their demands. The money is in a bag in the back seat. Stay *low*. Do you understand? Pass that around to the others."

"I understand."

There was silence, and then Cliff's voice. "Maddie are you all right?"

Cliff. Maddie closed her eyes as emotion swelled within her. "Yes. We're all fine," she managed. She wanted so badly to tell him that "we" included his child, but she didn't. She would get out of this. They all would. And tonight she would tell him, just like she'd planned. And tomorrow would be her very first Mother's Day. Her hand went to her stomach once more, and she imagined the day in a few months when she'd feel their baby move for the first time. And then a few months later when she'd hold their child in her arms with Cliff's strong arms surrounding both of them.

"Is it coming?" Simon demanded.

"I see it," Deek yelled.

Her hand tightened on the phone because she knew he was about to tell her to hang up. "I love you," she whispered into the phone, and Simon heard her.

"Who are you talking to?" he yelled.

"I love you, too. We're going to get y'all out of there. Just do what they tell you."

"Maddie." It was Sheriff Brady. "Tell them they're free to go. But, Maddie, be ready."

"They said you're free to go," she said, as Simon glared at her. "Money's in the backseat in a bag."

He grabbed the phone. "You keep everybody back. Or Maddie here will be the first to bite the dust," he yelled, then hung up and grabbed her by the collar and shoved her in front of him. She stumbled and turned toward him.

She hadn't even had to make a case for them to take her. God had worked it out for her. "Y'all stay calm," she said to the others as he shoved her shoulder and she stumbled back toward the door. The pregnancy test slipped from her waistband and hit the floor.

"You're not taking Maddie with you." Adela

moved forward. "You boys need to give yourselves up. This is not going to turn out good. God made you for more than this," she pleaded. "Give yourselves up. It's not too late."

"That's right," Esther Mae agreed. "Let us go, and things will be better for you. God will forgive yo-"

"Shut up." Simon pointed his gun at Esther Mae. "Red, you're going to be the first one I shoot."

Esther Mae stopped chomping on her gum. "Well, and here I thought we were bonding."

Maddie almost laughed. Esther Mae was one feisty woman, but she wished that for now she'd just stay quiet. But she knew that Red, as Simon had called her, was trying to once again distract them with her rambling.

"Take me with you, but let them go," Maddie said.

Simon's eyes hardened, and he yanked her around and locked his arm around her neck. Maddie didn't fight for fear he'd really shoot Esther Mae.

"We're not letting anyone go. Everyone get in the office, or I shoot Maddie right here and take the girl."

Jessie shoved Lizzie behind him. "Come on, man. Let the women go."

"I'm claustrophobic," Esther Mae squealed. "Norma, tell them, I can't go in that tiny room. I just can't do it. Norma Sue, *don't* let them put me in a closet." Suddenly Esther Mae made an awful noise and started choking. She grabbed her throat, her eyes grew wide, and she spun, then staggered one way, then the other, and then zigzagged toward Deek.

Instead of helping assist Esther Mae, Adela pushed the horrified teens back toward the end of the row of gum as her buddies made all kinds of commotion.

"Hold still, Esther I'll help you," Norma Sue hollered and grabbed Esther Mae in the Heimlich maneuver position and began hoisting her up and down, They looked like the choking scene in the movie *Mrs. Doubtfire* with all of their weaving and jumping.

It happened fast, and Maddie was stunned because she was also being strangled by Simon's elbow to her windpipe.

"Help, help," Norma Sue cried in a very unlike Norma Sue hysteria as she yanked hard and Esther Mae spit a huge wad of gum straight into Deek's face. It hit him in the cheek, and then Norma Sue rammed him like a linebacker blindsiding the quarterback.

And suddenly Maddie realize this was the sign. Holy smokin' fiasco! It had all been fake! Maddie reacted instantly. She stomped down hard onto Simon's flimsy running shoe. It was no protection from her hard-heeled boot. He screamed as the crack of toes breaking sounded from his foot. In the same instant, Maddie rammed her elbow hard into his ribcage while simultaneously throwing her head back to hit him in the jaw with the back of her head. She'd been head-butted by more cows than she could count and knew the technique well. He was yelling as he stumbled back. She spun and grabbed the wrist of the hand holding the gun with both her hands, All she was thinking as she hiked a knee upward with all her might was Simon was not going to hurt her friends. Or her baby.

Her knee hit its target. He crumbled forward, and his hold loosened on the gun. She fought him for it.

And then he pulled the trigger.

CHAPTER SEVEN

When the shot rang out inside the Sip-N-Go, Cliff bolted. "Maddie!"

Breaking past the cops, he raced toward the side of building. He could hear Rafe and Brady yelling his name, but he didn't stop. He flattened himself to the side of the wall and saw the cops in action mode, as the men he hadn't even realized were on the roof repelled down and slammed through the plate glass. It shattered into millions of pieces as they dropped to the ground. Chaos happened over the next few seconds as Cliff followed the team inside.

First thing he heard as he entered was a male cursing and screaming.

First thing he saw was a man splayed out on his belly, flattened to the ground like a pancake, his arms outstretched and Esther Mae sitting on his back. He was grunting but not the screamer. Norma Sue held a shotgun on him.

Second thing he saw was Adela and two teenagers emerging from behind the gum aisle looking scared but unharmed.

He spun the other direction, desperate to find Maddie. One of the officers was leaning over the counter, and that was where all the sound was coming from.

And then he heard her. "I need paramedics. Now! And stop your yelling. You did this, buster, and better you than any of my friends."

"You did this. You shot me."

"Oh, hush. It's just a flesh wound, you baby."

Cliff rounded the counter, and his heart started beating again when he saw Maddie. She had the unhappy thug on his stomach, and she had a knee jammed in his back, and she'd pulled one of his legs back as if she were about to hog tie a calf. The man squirmed, trying to get free, but Cliff had news for the guy. If Maddie had him like that, he wasn't going anywhere.

There was a trickle of blood on the ground dripping from the end of the man's shoe.

The deputy grinned at her. "Paramedics are coming through the door. You did good, Maddie."

"Thanks," she said, glancing at the deputy and then at Cliff. She looked tired, and she was a little green, but her smile exploded across her face as their eyes met.

"Maddie—"

"Hey there, cowboy. It's about time you showed up. Me and the Posse over there had to round up these ornery bulls all by our lonesome."

"Believe me I got here as soon as I could. But looks like you got it handled. Are you all right" He wanted to engulf her in his arms but she was a little tied up.

The man on the ground cursed and yelled. "I'm bleeding here. Get her off me!"

Maddie dug her knee harder into his back and bent his leg more. "It doesn't f eel so good to be my hostage does it?" She was all business now. "It's all about choices. And you made a very bad one. And literally shot yourself in the foot."

"That's the dad-gum truth," Norma Sue called from across the room. Police were handcuffing her victim and leading him out.

Esther Mae was grinning and hugging Adela and the two teens.

"This has been a very exciting day," she exclaimed. "And everyone is safe."

Paramedics arrived and moments later Maddie moved out of their way and came to Cliff. He engulfed her in a hug, clinging to her. The room was swarming with people now. The Posse's husbands arrived, and everyone was hugging, and people Cliff assumed were the teens' parents were with them, and Cliff was glad for everyone. But his focus was all on Maddie.

"I thought I might lose you," he managed, kissing her head, letting their hearts beat together as he just held onto her. "Are you hurt?"

"Nope, not going anywhere. And no worse off than a day wrestling cattle," she said, looking up at him, her eyes bright with tears. "I am so glad to see you."

When he saw those tears, pain sliced through him. "Don't cry." He pushed hair back from her face, then kissed her lips gently.

"It's just," she said. "I have something—"

"Maddie," Brady said coming up and looking apologetic. "I hate to break y'all up, but we need to get some statements. Sorry. Austin will take yours, if you don't mind."

Frustration crossed her face, and Cliff didn't want to let her go, but the sooner she gave her statement, the sooner he could take her home. "It's okay."

"Fine," she said, taking a deep breath. "And then I have something to tell you."

He dropped a kiss to her lips. "Sounds like a plan."

The last thing Maddie wanted to do was answer

questions. She wanted Cliff to herself so she could tell him he was going to be a daddy.

She started to move away from him, but the deputy took out his pad. "I can ask my questions right here. No need for you to leave," he said to Cliff.

"Great." Cliff kept his arm draped over her shoulders protectively.

Maddie loved the support she felt in his presence and wrapped an arm around his waist, so very thankful to have him in her life. She smiled at the deputy. "I need to thank you for being the calm voice in this nightmare." She held out her hand, and they shook briefly.

"Me? You were the one who did great. You kept your head in a time when most people would have lost their cool."

That almost made her laugh, thinking back to Esther Mae and Norma Sue. "Everyone in here kept their head on straight. Even when I thought some of them had lost their minds, turns out they knew exactly what they were doing." She laughed replaying Esther Mae and Norma Sue's award-winning act.

Austin pulled out his pad and gave her a grin. "So let's talk about that," he said with that same confident, sincere voice of his.

"Yes, let's do that," she said, and answered every question he had for her. The nightmare was over, her friends were safe, and this had been the longest morning of her life.

Thankfully the morning sickness had passed, and she now felt pretty good.

Excellent, actually, as Austin's pen paused.

"So that's it," he said. "I think we're through."

"Yes, all done. Now." She looked up at Cliff. "Let's get out of here. I have been waiting all day to tell you something—"

"Maddie," Jessie interrupted as he leaned down and picked something up off the tile floor. His expression was bright. "Wow, after all that happened, I completely forgot about this. Congratulations." He held out the the pregnancy test and grinned at Clint. "To you, too, sir."

Maddie stared at the test, and Cliff stared at her, and then at the test she held in her hands.

"Is that..." he started, his voice hushed. "Are we?"

She'd wanted so much to break the news to him when they were alone. But now, Maddie laughed and held the test out to him. "Congratulations, Mr. Masterson. You're officially a daddy now. And in nine months, we'll get to hold our precious baby in our arms at last." Tears welled in her eyes. She'd waited so very long to say these words. To feel this emotion and, after today, she knew even more certainly how very precious life was.

Cliff's eyes warmed and his cautious smile widened into the sexy grin that had always melted her heart. And then he whooped and scooped her up into his arms. "I'm going to be a daddy," he announced to everyone, and then he kissed her as everyone around them cheered and clapped.

But Maddie didn't really hear that much of it. She just wrapped her arms around her cowboy's neck, held on with all her might and kissed him with all her heart.

They were having a baby, and they were together. And that was all she'd ever wanted or needed.

Dear Reader,

Thank you for reading Maddie's Secret Baby, book 7 in the New Horizon Ranch Series. I've enjoyed each story in this series and loved intertwining the laugh out loud moments with the deep touching moments of the stories. I write stories that leave you with a smile and I love every minute of it. I hope you're smiling right now!

If you haven't read the other stories, I hope you will. If you've enjoyed this book, I would be so grateful if you could leave a review.

Join my newsletter at www.debraclopton.com
for all the news and special opportunities.

Thank you and happy reading!

Debra Clopton

New Horizon Ranch Series

Her Texas Cowboy (Book 1)

Five ranch-hands inherit a Texas ranch from their boss. These cowboys and cowgirl vow to honor their beloved boss by making the New Horizon Ranch the success he envisioned when he chose to leave his legacy in their care. Along the way they each find the love of a lifetime. You'll fall in love with these fun, sweet, emotional love stories.

Cowboy Cliff Masterson saw a woman in need and stepped in—because Maddie was too stubborn to ask…

Cowgirl Maddie Rose has never belonged anywhere but she's just inherited part of New Horizon Ranch—along with her partners, four handsome, extremely capable cowboys… Maddie's trying to adjust to her new life and her new partners she's still unable to believe she's an owner of this fabulous ranch. Not sure why she was included, she's out to prove herself worthy of the honor of the inheritance. Loving her new life in the small Texas town of Mule Hollow, she's determined that, for the first time in her life, she's going to finally belong somewhere...

Professional Bull Rider Cliff Masterson has been chasing his dreams for years—or has he been running from his past? He's searching for more in life and ready to dig in his spurs and put down roots deep in the heart of Texas. Rescuing a beautiful cowgirl from being trampled by a bull has him dreaming of romance, home and hearth.

But Maddie's had enough people in her life leave and she's not willing to risk her heart on him— Sparks fly as he's determined to prove to the feisty cowgirl that the only think he's chasing now is wedding bells with her...

Can the Matchmakin' Posse of Mule Hollow help this couple find their happily ever after?

Rafe (Book 2)

When runaway bride, Sadie Archer's car breaks down on the outskirts of Mule Hollow, Texas, she's not exactly dressed to fix the blown tire. Then again, she hadn't planned on this road trip or her life falling apart a week before her wedding. But now that she's hit the road, destination unknown, Sadie's decided it's time to disappear for a while and find out exactly what it is she wants out of life. But first she needs to change her flat tire and that is easier said than done when one is wearing...

A bunny suit!

Ex-cowboy star Rafe Masterson thinks he's seeing things at first but yes—that is definitely a female head sticking out of the furry white bunny suit, tangling with a spare tire. A cowboy who guards his heart carefully, he's still always willing to help someone in need...even one wearing white fur from top to bottom. Completely captivated by the unusual woman, Rafe senses she's in trouble in more ways than the flat tire. He's part owner of the New Horizon Ranch and offers her a job as cook—even though they don't need a cook.

Sadie accepts even though she can't really cook but this is the perfect answer to her needs right now...and how hard can it be anyway?

These two might be down-on-love but love hasn't

given up on them and the Matchmaking Posse of Mule Hollow has just gotten them in their sights...

Chase (Book 3)

Being a bridesmaid at her best friend's wedding in the sleepy town of Mule Hollow Texas is the perfect place for Amber Rivers to lay low to avoid a stalker hot on her heels back in Houston. She loves her job and her city life and isn't looking to stay long in the country-but she's blindsided by her attraction to the self-assured rancher, Chase Hartley...

Chase agrees to watch over socialite Amber while his partner heads off on his honeymoon but despite the high voltage sparks lighting up between them he has no intention of getting any closer to Amber than necessary to keep her safe. But he soon realizes there's a whole lot more to Amber than he first assumed and keeping his distance is becoming harder with every passing moment they're together.

An outside threat plus a little friendly tampering from the meddling Matchmakin' Posse of Mule Hollow puts this couple on high alert as they try not to fall in love.

Ty (Book 4)

Best friends forever...happily ever that is...Christmas wedding bells will be ringing if the Matchmakin' Posse of Mule Hollow can get this stubborn cowboy and cowgirl together under the mistletoe for the most anticipated kiss of the holiday.

Will Ty Calder, mild mannered partner in the New Horizon Ranch, get his secret Christmas wish and heal his lonesome heart this season? Find out in Book 4 of the New Horizon Ranch/Mule Hollow series.

Horse trainer Ty Calder did the right thing four years ago and sent his best friend, Mia Shaw off with a hug and best wishes in her quest for her rodeo dreams to come true. But now she's back for the Christmas holiday and he's not sure he can send her off again without revealing his true feelings...

Mia is back in Mule Hollow healing up from an injury that could end her run for the championship. But, lately her heart's not been completely committed to her rodeo dreams and Ty has her thinking he might just be the reason.

Suddenly, tensions are running high between Mia and Ty...sparks are flying and have been spotted by the Matchmakin' Posse. Now these two are dodging mistletoe, matchmakers and the kiss they're both fighting to avoid and longing for.

But Ty can't believe Mia is ready to give up on her dreams when she's so close...he knows it means more to her than most people realize. No matter how much he wants a life with Mia he refuses to stand in the way of her dreams even if it means losing her forever...

It may take his four partners at the New Horizon Ranch and the town of Mule Hollow to get these two believing Christmas is especially the time that love can conquer all.

This is going to be one Christmas these two will remember forever...

Dalton (Book 5)

Dalton Borne is a cowboy who keeps his past closed

up inside. He's watched his partners at the New Horizon Ranch find love and he's happy for them and even envious. But his past prevents him from believing he deserves a future that includes a love of his own. But then one stormy night he rescues a very pregnant Rae Anne Tyson from floodwaters and ends up delivering her baby on the side of the road. Suddenly Dalton's life is turned upside down and no matter what he believes he does or doesn't deserve—he can't walk away from helping Rae Anne.

Treb (Book 6)

Former special ops soldier Treb Carson has returned to his ranching roots joining up with the New Horizon Ranch. Afghanistan and the loss of his brother have him ready to move forward into happier times–he's looking for love and to start a family. He's not expecting to be captivated by Megan Tanner, the completely wrong woman for his plans. The workaholic, new veterinarian in town doesn't have marriage on her agenda and she's made that clear, but he can't get her or the kiss they share off his mind.

Megan Tanner has her personal reasons for not believing in happily-ever-after, but now she's moved to the hometown of the Matchmakin' Posse of Mule Hollow. Avoiding their antics is easy for now, it's calving season and that means no time for anything but work and building her vet practice. But then she's blindsided by the smokin'-hot, ex-military cowboy and the immediate sparks she can't deny or the kiss she can't forget.

Treb knows all the reasons why Megan isn't the woman for him…but he can't seem to stop himself. Now he's determined to find out why Megan is so against falling in love and proving to her that she can trust him with her heart.

And he's got a certain three nosey ladies on his side…can the "Posse" help this couple find their happily-ever-after?

More Books by Debra Clopton

Mule Hollow Matchmakers Series

The Trouble with Lacy Brown (Book 1)

And Baby Makes Five (Book 2)

The Men of Mule Hollow Series

Her Forever Cowboy (Book 1)

Cowboy for Keeps (Book 2)

Yuletide Cowboy (Book 3)

The Cowboys of Sunrise Ranch

Her Unforgettable Cowboy (Book 1)

Her Unexpected Cowboy (Book 2)

Her Unlikely Cowboy (Book 3)

For the complete list, visit her website

www.debraclopton.com

Made in the US.
Middletown, DE
10 April 2017